To my dad, who taught me everything I know about whopper-sized fish tales.
– S.N.

For Lucy
– B.C.

First Edition 2011
Kane Miller, A Division of EDC Publishing

Text copyright © Stacy Nyikos, 2010
Illustrations copyright © Bret Conover, 2010

For information contact:
Kane Miller, A Division of EDC Publishing
PO Box 470663
Tulsa, OK 74147-0663
www.kanemiller.com
www.edcpub.com

Library of Congress Control Number: 2010921033

Manufactured by Regent Publishing Services, Hong Kong
Printed November 2010 in ShenZhen, Guangdong, China

1 2 3 4 5 6 7 8 9 10

ISBN: 978-1-935279-64-8

ROPE 'EM!

Written by Stacy Nyikos • Illustrated by Bret Conover

Kane Miller
A DIVISION OF EDC PUBLISHING

Scout and Virgil were the O.K. Coral's best cowhands ever.
Scout could herd any fish – feisty, frisky, even ferocious.

And Virgil could rope and tie one in six seconds flat.

Yes, sir, they were the best. Especially at outdoing each other.

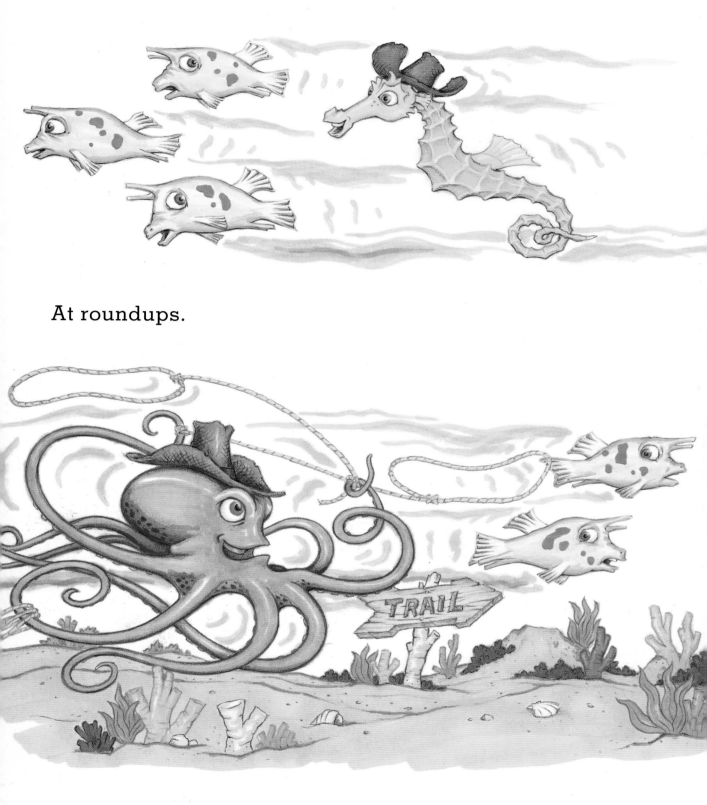

At roundups.

On the trail.

Even at branding time. That left a mark!

Until one day when trouble arrived. Big trouble. The kind that starts with "T" rhymes with "B" and stands for Bullface. Barrier Reef Bullface. Biggest, meanest, hungriest bull shark for miles around.

The outlaw appeared out of nowhere. Before a single cowpoke could bar the gate, the shark stampeded through. Smashed up a pen. And began chomping down a school of cowfish, horns and all.

Scout slammed on his hat. "I'll herd that lowdown, good-for-nuthin' outlaw right off the reef. Nobody messes with the O.K. Coral. Nobody."

"Couldn't have said it better myself." Virgil grabbed his eight best lassoes. "Except, he needs to be roped."

Scout's eyes narrowed.

"Herded." "Roped." "Herded! " "Roped!!! "

"Dabnubbit, can't an outlaw eat in peace?" Bullface lunged after another mouthful of cowfish.

Scout galloped to catch up. "I'll get him!"

"I'll get him!" Virgil charged, his lassoes twirling.

The only thing Scout got was one of Virgil's lassoes around his tail. He floundered, flipped and flopped into the octopus. The two rolled head over fin right into the Bull's...

"Eye! My eye!" Bullface grabbed his eye. He yowled. He moaned. He crashed through the bunkhouse, the fence and the gate, and then tumbled right off the ledge.

"I'll be back," he called. "And I'm eating you two first."

Scout yanked Virgil's rope off his tail. "Lasso-twirling yoyo. Because of you, we lost him."

"Me?" Virgil pulled Scout's hat off his head. "I would have done just fine without you. Big greenhorn."

The seahorse's tail uncurled. "Who are you calling green, pardner?"

"Pardner?" The octopus laughed so hard, he inked. "Let the best cowhand handle this."

Scout squared his hat. "I mean to."

Scout was up at dawn. It was early. Mighty early. But not early enough. Virgil's bed was already empty.

Scout raced toward the gate. "Roped 'em!" Virgil called out.

"Oh, you roped him all right. Reckon you can stop him?"

"'Course I can stop him." Virgil pulled hard on the lassoes. "Stop."

Bullface grinned a dastardly grin. He stopped all right. Virgil landed sunny-side up on the shark's back.

Bullface went wild. He bucked like a bull at a rodeo.

"Heeeeeelp!!!!!!!!!!!!!!!!!" Virgil yodeled.

"I'm just a greenhorn," Scout said.

"I take that back. You're good! Real good!" Virgil squeaked.

Scout leaned forward. "Good?"

"You're the best herder ever!"

"Now you're talking." Scout squared his hat. Curled up his tail. Shot forward like a runaway torpedo.

He herded Bullface up one side of the flats and back down the other.

Over mountains and across ravines.

"Stop him already," Virgil said.

"I'm working on it." Scout dipped and dove. He charged and drove.

But no matter how hard he tried, he couldn't herd Bullface. He couldn't even wear the bandit out. He only wore himself out. Finally, he stopped.

Bullface did too.

"About time." Virgil shimmied off of Bullface's back. The wily old bandit didn't even notice. He began to circle Scout like a chuckwagon at…

"Chowtime!" Bullface lunged. Scout tried to gallop away, but the outlaw nabbed his tail.

"Heeeeeelp!!!!!!!!!!!!!!!" Scout yodeled.

"I'm just a lasso-twirling yoyo," Virgil said.

Scout wiggled. He squirmed. Bullface began to suck him
down like a long, cold drink of water on a hot, sunny day.

"You're the best roper ever!!!!!" Scout cried out.

"That's more like it."

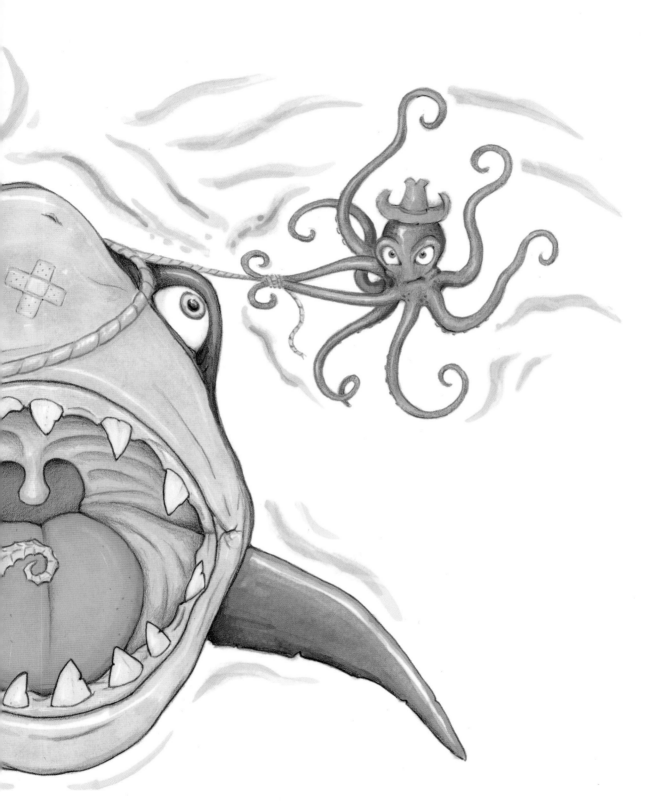

Faster than a spiny dogfish chasing his tail, Virgil threw a lasso around Bullface's snout and pulled.

Bullface roared.

Scout went sailing through the water head over tail.

Over tail.

Over head.

"You going to somersault around all day or are you going to help me?" Virgil said.

Over head.

Over…

"I never thought you'd ask." Scout skidded to a stop.
"Charge!"

Scout and Virgil charged
all right. Only this time
they charged together.

The outlaw never knew
what hit him. There were
fins to the left of him.
Lassoes to the right. And
Bullface was stuck smack-
dab in the middle."

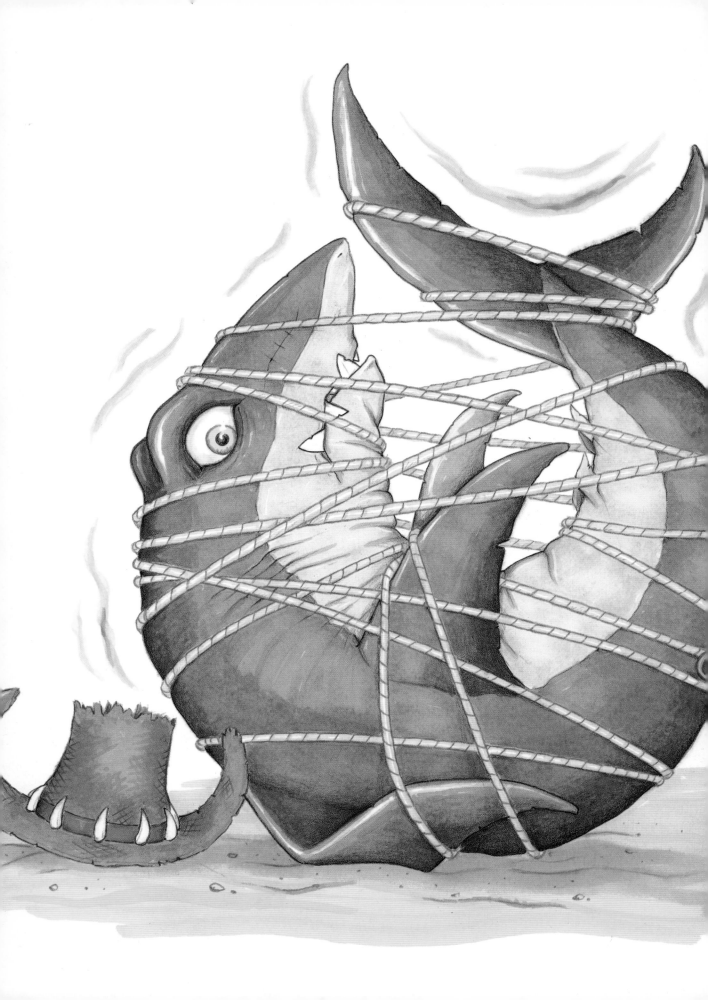

Together, Scout and Virgil corralled the bandit in five seconds flat. It was a new record.

Virgil looked at Scout. Scout looked at Virgil. They both looked at the bandit, wound up tighter than a roll of sushi.

"Not bad herding…for a greenhorn," Virgil said.

"Pretty good roping…for a yoyo," Scout replied.

Slowly, Virgil stuck out a tentacle. "Pardner?"

"Pardner!"

By sundown, news of Scout and Virgil's deed had grown three times the size of even the biggest fish tale.

They weren't just the O.K. Coral's best cowhands. They were
its best team, too.

Well, most of the time…